Our Little Swiss Cousin

Mary Hazelton Blanchard Wade

Our Little Swiss Cousin

CHAPTER I

CARL'S HOLIDAY

"To-morrow, to-morrow!" Carl kept repeating to himself.

He was standing at the window of the little cottage and looking out toward the great mountain. He had lived under its shadow all his life. Its snowy summit was coloured a fiery red as it stood against the sky in the sunset light. People in far-away lands would give a great deal to see such a glorious sight.

But Carl saw another picture in his mind. It was the grand procession of the next day, that would celebrate the close of school before the summer vacation. Thousands of children would march in the line. They would carry the flag of Switzerland,—the white cross on a red ground. It was the emblem of their country's freedom, and they loved it well.

There would be bands of music; there would be a speech by the mayor of the city. Feasts would be spread, to which all the children were invited. Yes, the glorious day was near, and Carl was very happy.

"Carl, my boy, are you thinking of the good time to-morrow?" said a voice at the other side of the room.

Carl started, and, turning round, he saw his father standing in the doorway.

"O father, is that you? How glad I am to see you!" and the little boy rushed into the good man's arms.

"Yes, I am all ready for the festival. Mother has my best clothes laid out on the bed. She is planning to go, too, and now you are home just in time to go with us. I am very, very glad." Carl was so excited that he talked faster than usual.

"I am tired of working in a hotel in the city, the country is so much pleasanter," answered his father. "And now I shall spend the summer with your mother and you. The people of the village wish me to take the cows to the mountain pasture. You shall go, too, and we will have a good time together."

"That will be fine. I never spent the whole summer there before. How soon are we to start, father?"

"Next week. The days are growing warmer and the flowers must already be in bloom upon the Alps. But now we must see your mother and talk about to-morrow. On my way home I heard in the village that you were going to the festival. Nearly all the neighbours are going too, aren't they?"

At this moment the door opened and a kind-faced woman came in, bringing a pail of milk in each hand. Her eyes were as blue as the sky, and her hair was nearly as fair as Carl's. It was easy to see that she was the boy's mother.

A happy smile lighted her face when she saw who was in the room. It was as much a surprise to her as it had been to Carl. She supposed her husband was still working in the big hotel at Lucerne, where so many strangers came from other lands.

When her husband told her of the work he had been doing, the heavy trunks which he had to lift till his back had grown lame, her face grew full of pity.

"It was too hard for you, Rudolf," she cried. "It is far better for you to take care of the cows this summer. We will go with you, Carl and I, and we shall have a merry time."

She moved quickly about the room as she strained the milk into the crocks and made ready the simple supper. In a few minutes the little family gathered around the table. There was sweet, fresh milk from the cows. There was the black rye bread which Carl had been used to eating all his life,—indeed, he had never seen white bread in his home. Besides these, there was a round cheese, from which each one cut a slice as he wished.

Best of all, there was a sort of cake made of dough and chopped dried fruits. Apples and cherries and almonds were all mixed in this cake and Carl thought it was very nice. It was put on the table to-night in honour of his father's home-coming.

Night after night Carl had a supper like this. Morning after morning, the breakfast was the same. The only difference was that sometimes there was the cake with the dried fruits.

Yet Carl was very happy and healthy. To be sure, he had meat and coffee for dinner only once a week. This was on Sunday. It was no wonder that he looked forward to that day as the best of all, for it seemed a feast day to him. At the noon meal on other days there was only soup or potatoes with the bread and cheese. There was little change through the year except at the time when the fruit and nuts were ripe and they could be eaten fresh.

After the supper was over, the family sat a while longer around the table and talked about the school festival. Carl's father had just come from Lucerne. He told the boy how the buildings were decorated. He named the bands that would furnish the music.

"I am to march, father," Carl said. "And I am to carry the flag of my country. Children from all the villages around the lake are to take part, I hear. Just think! although we are back in the country, our school has its place in the procession."

Carl's mother showed her husband the bright red skirt that she was going to wear. It would reach to the tops of her shoes. There was a white waist with big sleeves that she had starched and ironed. There was a new black bodice she had just made; it would be laced about the waist, and it fitted her finely. She had polished the bands of silver to fasten across the back of her head above the long braids of glossy hair. She would certainly look very well in her finery, and her husband would be proud of her. Oh, yes, that was certain.

What kind of a hat would she wear? None at all! There was no need, and it would be a shame to hide the silver bands; they were too pretty. What did it matter if some of the women of Switzerland dressed like the people of other lands? Carl's mother was not ready to follow new fashions yet awhile. The old customs of her village were good enough for her.

It was a small room where Carl and his parents sat and talked. Everything was fresh and clean; the floor had been scrubbed so that no spot could be seen upon it. The table was unpainted. The chairs had straight, stiff backs; no rocking-chair or lounge had ever found a place here. Carl's mother had never rested herself on such a piece of furniture in her life.

There was one strange-looking object in the room. It was large and white. It reached far up toward the ceiling, and was made of porcelain. It was the family stove. It had belonged to Carl's great-grandfather, and had stood in this very place, summer and winter, for a hundred years at least. It would not seem like home without it.

When baby Carl was first old enough to notice things around him, he used to creep up to the stove and try to touch the pictures painted on its sides. One was the scene of a battle where the Swiss were driving their enemies down a mountain. On the other side, a hunter was painted. He was bringing home a chamois that hung from his shoulders.

When the boy grew older, he used to climb the steps that led up to the top of the stove. It was so nice and warm there behind the curtains that hung from the ceiling down to the front edge. It made a cosy little room where Carl could lie and warm himself after a walk in the winter air. Sometimes the boy slept there all night long; but that was only in the coldest weather.

In the daytime his mother often put her fruit there to dry, or perhaps she hung wet clothes there. It had many uses.

There were no real stairs in the house. There was an upper room, however, and when a person wished to enter it he must first climb on top of the stove and then pass through a hole in the ceiling. It was a strange way of building the house; don't you think so?

Perhaps you wonder that Carl did not get burned when he lay on top of the stove. That was because there was never any fire in it! This probably seems the strangest thing about it, but you must understand that the fire was built in a sort of furnace out in the hall. The heat passed from this furnace into the porcelain stove, so it was not unpleasantly warm when one touched it.

After talking a while with his father, Carl climbed up to the top of the stove, and creeping through the hole in the ceiling, he entered his bedroom. He quickly said his prayers and then jumped into bed. He must get to sleep as early as possible, for he would be called before daybreak. At least, his mother promised to call him, but she did not need to do so,—he was the first one in the house to wake.

"Father! mother!" he shouted, before the clock cried "cuckoo," three times.

It was none too early; lights moving from room to room could already be seen in the neighbours' houses. The whole village was astir.

There was a walk of several miles for all who were going to the celebration. This walk would bring them to the shores of the lake. A steamer would be waiting at the pier to take them across to the city of Lucerne on the other side. A party of merry people moved along the road just as the sunrise coloured the mountain-tops. Every one was dressed in his Sunday best.

There were many little girls, all in white, their yellow hair hanging in long braids. Some of them had immense wreaths of flowers or laurel leaves to carry in the procession, but the flags were carried by the boys.

See! there is the beautiful lake just ahead. How blue its waters are! The shadows of lofty mountains can be seen if you look down upon the clear surface. Brave men have lived on its shores. Noble deeds have been done near by. Every Swiss loves this lake, as he thinks of the history of his country.

The little steamer was quickly loaded with its gay passengers, and made its way over the waters. Other steamers soon came in sight, but all were moving in the same direction,—toward the city of Lucerne.

Such a festival is not held every year. Each village generally celebrates the close of school by a picnic or steamer-ride. There is usually something pleasant for the children, but not always a time like this.

When the day was over, it was hard for Carl to tell what he had enjoyed most. In the morning, after the children had marched around the city to lively music, they went out to a large open space where the feast was served. Every one had all the coffee and cakes he wished. There were many odd little cakes that only Swiss women know how to make. The children enjoyed them hugely.

After the feast games were played, and there were rides on the flying horses. You will laugh when you hear the name of one of the games. It is "Blind Cow." Carl is very fond of it. It is much like our "Blind Man's Buff." Carl and his friend Franz chose one corner of a large field. Marie, Franz's sister, and Freda, another little friend, were with them. They were soon joined by other children, and they had a lively game.

Carl was the cow oftener than any one else. He didn't care. It was great fun stumbling around with blinded eyes, and trying to catch the others. When they thought they were quite safe and out of reach, one of them was sure to laugh and show where he was. Then Carl would make a sudden spring, and catch the laugher.

Before the afternoon was over, the mayor spoke to the children about the kind teacher who had helped not only the Swiss, but children all over the world. That teacher's name was Pestalozzi. Carl knew the story well, but he loved to hear it over and over again.

More than a hundred years ago there was a good man who lived in Switzerland very near Carl's house. It was a time of war. Soldiers from other countries had chosen Switzerland for their battle-field. They took possession of the homes of the people. They destroyed their crops. They ate their supplies of food. The Swiss suffered greatly. After these enemies had gone away, they found themselves poor, and many of them were starving.

Pestalozzi was not a rich man, but his heart was filled with pity. He went among the poor and gave them all he had. He was especially fond of the children. He cared for them as well as he could; he got them bread to eat and clothes to wear; best of all, he taught them and kept their minds busy. But at last his money was all spent. What could he do now?

He gathered the ragged, hungry boys around him. They had grown to love him, and were willing to do anything he directed. He showed them how to sew and spin and do many other kinds of work. They were soon able to earn enough money to support themselves and their school.

Pestalozzi did not teach in the way others did. He said:

"It is not enough for these children to study their lessons from books and then be whipped if they do not get them. They must see how real things are; they must study from objects. The living birds and flowers should help them. They must learn to shape things for themselves, and see as much as possible with their own eyes. Then they will love to study; they will enjoy their schools, and be happiest when there."

He set a new fashion for the world. His pupils learned so fast and well that other teachers came to watch and learn his ways. His fame spread to other countries, to England and America. They also copied his manner of teaching. Not only Swiss children, but those of different lands, began to enjoy their schools better. It all came about through the kind and loving work of Pestalozzi.

Carl has never known of a boy being whipped in his school. Such a punishment is seldom given in Switzerland. The teacher tries love and kindness first. If these fail, the boy is turned out of school. It is a terrible disgrace; it will follow the boy all his life, and he dreads it above everything.

After the mayor had spoken of Pestalozzi to the children, he bade them be proud of their schools and their school-buildings, which were finer than even the council-houses. He told them to be glad that all children of Switzerland, no matter how poor they were, could go to these schools and learn of the great world around them.

As he spoke, he could see in the faces of thousands of little ones that they were proud indeed.

Carl whispered to Franz, who stood beside him:

"There is no country like ours, is there, Franz? We could not be happy anywhere else, I'm sure."

His friend replied, "No, indeed, Carl. It is the home of free men, and we must grow up to keep it so. I don't care if we do have to study for six hours every school-day. We learn all the faster and, besides, we have ever so many holidays."

The best part of the holiday came in the evening, for that was the time for fireworks. There was a grand display on the shore of the lake. There were rockets, and Roman candles, and fire-pictures, and many other beautiful pieces which lighted the sky and were reflected in the waters of the lake. Many of the people watched the display from the decks of the little steamers, which were also bright with coloured lights.

The time came all too soon for the homeward journey.

"What a lovely time I've had," sighed Carl, as he reached his own door. "I only wish it were going to be to-morrow instead of to-day."

"It was a fine show indeed," said his father. "Everybody looked well and happy. But I must say that I liked the dress of the people of our own village better than that of any other."

CHAPTER II

THE MOUNTAIN PASTURE

"Here, Carl, take this kettle, and you, Franz, may carry the other," said Carl's mother.

It was two days after the school holiday, and again the village was astir before sunrise. There was a great jingling of cow-bells as the men and boys moved about from farm to farm and gathered the cattle together.

Rudolf was to take all the cows in the village to the mountain pastures for the summer. Carl and his friend Franz would help him in taking care of them. Carl's mother would make the cheese. In the autumn, they would bring the cows back and divide the cheese according to the number of cows each family owned.

It was a joyful time and well deserving a holiday. Almost every one in the village would keep the herder and his family company on his way up the mountainside. Their food and cooking dishes must be carried; the cows must be kept in the right path, while their friends, who were leaving them for months, must be cheered and kept in good heart.

At last everything was made ready. Brown Katze, the handsomest cow in the village, led the line. She tossed her head as though she could already sniff the fresh air of the uplands. How the bells jingled! What gay songs rang out! Carl was a fine singer himself, and if you listened you could hear his voice above all the rest.

The procession at first followed a narrow path through the woods. There were many beech and chestnut trees where Carl would go nutting in the fall. After a while these were left behind, and evergreens were the only trees to be seen.

It was already growing cooler and the cows pushed onward. They seemed to know of the pleasure before them,—the sweet grass and herbs which they would soon be able to eat to their hearts' content.

Ah! the woods came to an end at last, and the beautiful pastures were reached. There is nothing in the world like them. It is no wonder that the cheeses made here are noted all over the world.

Here were thousands of the lovely Alpine roses, royal red-purple in colour. Here too, harebells, violets, and pansies were growing wild. It was difficult to walk without stepping on some delicate, beautiful flower.

The party followed a narrow path through the meadow. They soon came to the little cottage where Carl would pass the summer. The building was broad and low, and had a wide, overhanging roof on which great rocks were lying, here and there. They were needed to keep it from blowing off during the hard storms of the winter.

Girl with chalet in background
THE CHALET.
Carl's father opened the door and looked carefully around to see if everything had remained safe since the summer before. Yes, it was all right; no one would know from the appearance that people had not been inside the room for eight months at least.

There was the stove over which the milk would be heated before it could be made into cheese. The rough table stood in the corner, while at the farther end was a supply of hay to be used in case the cattle had need of it.

It was a large room, but there were many low windows, so it would be bright and cheerful when the shutters had been taken down. Just back of this room was the stable, where the cows could find shelter at night.

Shouldn't you think Carl would be lonely here? No other houses could be seen, no matter in what direction he turned. He might not look upon any human faces except those of Franz and his father and mother for days at a time. In whatever way he might turn, his eyes would meet mountains,—mountains everywhere. But he loved to be here; he loved these mountains with all his heart. They gave him a feeling of freedom and of strength, and he would often say to himself:

"Ah! the good God has given us a wonderful world to live in, and we are a part of it all."

Day after day of the short summer Carl and Franz would drive the cows higher and higher in search of new feeding-grounds. At last they would come to the bare, brown rocks near the summit, and they would know that the season's work was nearly over.

The villagers who had come with the family had a picnic dinner at the chalet, as the Swiss call a mountain cottage like Carl's. Then a few songs were sung with a hearty good-will. The time passed so quickly that the people came near forgetting how late it was growing when one of the party, standing in the doorway, heard the clock strike four.

"Good friends, we must start homeward at once," he cried. "Think of the long climb down and the dark path through the woods."

What a bustle and commotion there was now! What hearty hand-shakings were given! Then away they went, calling back from time to time, or blowing another farewell upon their horns when they were hidden from sight by the trees below.

Carl and Franz turned to help Rudolf in the care of the cows, for the milking must be done before nightfall. Carl's mother made up fresh beds from the hay and put away the provisions. She would soon have plenty to do besides, for the cheese-making would be her work.

"Carl," she said to her boy that night, "you will be old enough to be a herder yourself before long. In four or five years you and Franz can bring the cows here to pasture by yourselves, and do all the work, too. You must learn how to make cheese this summer."

So it was that the two boys took their first lessons, and before many days they had become good helpers inside the house as well as outdoors.

They would lift the great kettles of milk and place them over the fire to heat. At just the right moment, the rennet must be put in to curdle the milk and separate the curds from the whey. Now for the beating with a clean pine stick. Carl's strong arms could aid his mother well in this work, upon which the goodness of the cheese depended.

"Well done," the herder's wife would say. "It is easy enough to make cheese with two such good lads to help me."

She was very fond of Franz, and loved him like a son. The faces of both boys grew bright when they were praised like this, and they were all the more eager to work. There was plenty to do yet, for the boiling and pressing must come next.

At last a big mould was ready to set away; but even now it must be watched and turned, day after day.

Carl's mother proudly watched her store grow larger as the weeks passed by. Those cheeses would bring large sums of money,—at least, it seemed so to her. But, of course, the money would be divided among the different families, according to the number of cows each sent to the pasture.

One morning as Carl was watching the herd, he looked down the mountainside and saw a party of strangers coming up the winding path. Then he heard a voice call:

"Hullo, hullo, little boy! Is your home near by? And can we get a little something to eat? We are very hungry."

It was a gentleman who spoke these words. A lady and a little girl about ten years old were with him. They looked like Americans. Carl had seen many strangers from other lands, and he said to himself:

"Yes, they must be Americans."

The little girl was very pretty, and she gave Carl a sweet smile when he ran to help her up over a rough place.

"Yes, sir, I'm sure my mother will welcome you," said our little Swiss cousin. "There she is, now." And he pointed to the cottage a short way off, where his mother sat knitting in the doorway.

When Carl went home to dinner an hour afterward, he found the strangers still there. They had lunched on bread and cheese and the rich sweet milk, and they declared they had never tasted anything nicer in their lives.

"Oh, my!" said the little girl, "I believe I was never so hungry in my life before."

"Carl," she went on, for his mother had told her his name, "do you ever carve little houses to look like this one? If you do, I will ask my father to buy one. He told me that Swiss boys do carve all sorts of things."

"I am sorry," answered Carl, "but I never did work of that kind. Over to the west of us are villages where every one carves. The men do so as well as the boys. One family will make the toy houses all their lives; another will carve chamois and nothing else; still another will cut out toy cows. But we in our village have other work."

"But why don't the wood-carvers change? I should think they would get tired of always doing the same thing," said Ruth, for this was the child's name.

"I suppose they never think about it. It is hard work living among these mountains of ours. People wish to earn all they can, and if one makes the same kind of thing, over and over again, he learns how to do it very quickly."

"I understand now," answered Ruth. "And I see, too, why the Swiss have such a queer way of making watches. One man in a village keeps making one part of the works; another man works steadily, year after year, on another part, and so on. All these different parts are sent to the factory in the city, and quickly put together into complete watches. That is what my father told me, and he must know, I'm sure."

"Yes, that is the work of the people around Geneva," answered Carl. "I have never been to that city yet, but I hope to go there before long."

"We stayed there a week. Nearly every one I met spoke in French, while you talk German all the time, Carl. That seems so queer. You live in the same country, and yet you speak in different languages. Why, father says we shall soon visit another part of Switzerland where I shall hear nothing but Italian."

"I suppose it must seem strange to you," replied Carl, thoughtfully, "yet we all love our country, and each other. We would fight promptly to save Switzerland, or to help any part in time of danger. We even have different religious beliefs; but while we of our village are Catholics, and try to do as the good priests tell us, there are many others not far away who are Protestants. Yet we are at peace with one another. Oh, I believe our country is the freest and best in all the world. Excuse me, please; I can't help thinking so."

Ruth laughed. "I like you all the better, Carl, for feeling in this way. Of course, I love America the best, and shall be glad to get home again after we have travelled awhile longer. But I think your country is the most beautiful I have ever seen. And father says we Americans can learn some good lessons from Switzerland. I shall understand more about that, however, when I am older."

"How long have you been here in Switzerland?" Carl asked.

"It is two months, I think. But we haven't been travelling all the time. Mother wasn't well and we stayed most of the time at the queerest place I ever heard of. This was so mother could drink the waters and get cured."

"Do you remember the name of the place?" asked Carl.

"Yes, it is called the Leuken Baths."

"I've often heard of those waters. They are boiling as they come bursting out of the ground, aren't they?"

"Yes, but that is not the odd part of it, because there are many other boiling springs in the world. It is the way that people are cured at these baths that made me laugh. Why, Carl, some of them stay in the water all day long! They wear flannel gowns and sit soaking while they play games on floating tables, and even eat their dinners there. The men smoke, while the women laugh and chat. The hot water brings out a rash all over the body, and the blood, after a while, becomes purer."

Carl laughed when he pictured the food on floating tables and people sitting around them with only heads and shoulders out of water.

"Did your mother do like these others?" he asked, and he turned his head toward the beautifully dressed lady who sat talking with his parents.

"No, she said that was too much, but she drank a good deal of the water, and she feels better than she has for years," replied Ruth.

"Come, come, my dear, we have stayed a long time. I fear we have kept these good people from their work. We must thank them, and go back to the town."

It was Ruth's father who said these words. He was standing in the doorway, and ready to start.

"I shall not forget you, Carl," said the little girl. "I shall often think of this little cottage up on the mountain, with the pretty flowers growing around it and the cows feeding near by."

After they had gone, Carl hastily picked a bunch of Alpine roses.

"She thought they were beautiful," he said to himself. "Perhaps she will press one of them, and keep it to remember me by."

Then with strong bounds and leaps the little boy overtook the party before they had gone very far. When he reached them, however, he was suddenly overcome with shyness. He hastily put the flowers into the hands of Ruth's mother, and was far away again before she could thank him.

"He is a dear little fellow," said the lady. "He will make a strong man, and a good one, too, I believe. We will always keep these beautiful flowers. Perhaps we may come here again in a year or two, Ruth. Then we can tell Carl how much we thought of his little gift."

CHAPTER III

THE SCHOOLMASTER'S VISIT

"Good news! good news!" cried Carl, as he came running into the house, quite out of breath.

"The schoolmaster is coming, mother. I know it must be he. Come, Franz, let's go to meet him."

The sun was just hiding his head behind the mountain-tops, and the little family were about to sit down to their evening meal.

"Do go at once, my dear boys," said Carl's mother. "Tell the good teacher how glad we are at his coming."

It was not a complete surprise, for the schoolmaster had promised Carl to spend a week with him on the mountain pastures, if it were possible.

Another place was quickly set at the table. In a few minutes the boys returned, and with them was a man with a kind face and a hearty voice.

"Welcome, welcome! my friend," said Rudolf. "It is indeed a pleasure to see you here. What news is there from the good folks of our village?"

"They are all well, and send greetings. Even poor little Gretel, the cretin, seemed to understand where I was coming, and she sent you her love."

What is a cretin, you wonder? A person of weak mind is so called in Switzerland. You often find such people who are not as bright as they should be. The mind is dull and dark, it cannot see and understand like others.

Why is it that cretins are often found in the homes of the poor? Some think it is because the Swiss are such hard workers, and yet do not have the nourishing food they should.

"Have you been at home all summer?" asked Rudolf.

"No, I had business that took me over the St. Bernard Pass. It was a hard journey, even in this summer-time, for I travelled most of the way on foot."

"O, how I wish I could have gone with you," cried Franz. "I have always longed to visit the good monks and see their brave dogs."

"It must be a terrible tramp over the mountain in winter," the schoolmaster went on. "Yet every year there are some people who need to go that way at that season. How much worse it would be, however, if the monastery were not there, with the priests living in it and giving their lives to help others."

"They say that the cold is so great that the monks cannot stand more than a few years of such a life," said Rudolf.

"It is true," replied the schoolmaster. "Many of them die before their time, while others must after a while go down to warmer lands. The noble dogs that they raise stand the cold much better."

"I have often made a picture for myself of a snow-storm on the St. Bernard," said Carl, thoughtfully. He had not spoken for a long time. "How the drifts pile up and fill the pathway. The snow falls thick and fast, and after a while the poor traveller cannot tell which way to turn. He grows cold and numb; he is quite tired out. At last he gives up hope, and perhaps he sinks down, and perhaps he loses all sense of where he is. Now is the very time that the good monks, watching the storm, loose the dogs. But first, food and reviving drink are fastened to the collars of the trusty animals.

"Off they bound, down the mountainside, scenting the air on every side. They understand their duty and work faithfully. They find the poor traveller in time to save his life and guide him to the home of the priests. Ah! how I love these good men and their faithful dogs."

"Your cheeks have grown quite rosy with the story, my boy," said the schoolmaster. "The picture in your mind must be bright, indeed. But we cannot praise too highly both the monks and their loving deeds. Sometimes, alas! the dogs do not find the travellers in time, however. Then they can only drag their dead bodies to the monastery, where they will stay till friends of the travellers come to claim them. But enough of this sad thought for to-night; let us talk of other things."

"Dear master," said Franz, "please tell us of other things you have seen this summer. We always love to hear your stories."

"Let me see. O, yes, now I think of something that will interest you boys. I travelled for quite a distance with a hunter. He had been in search of chamois, but he says they are getting very scarce now. He was bringing home only one."

Goat following boy
"'FOLLOWING ITS MASTER ABOUT JUST LIKE A DOG.'"
"It seems a shame to kill the poor creatures," said Carl's father. "They are gentle and harmless, and take pleasure in living where others find only danger. Once I came suddenly upon a herd of them. They seemed to be having a game of chase together, and were frolicking gaily. But at the sound of my footstep they fled like the wind over the snow and ice. In a moment, almost, they were out of sight."

"Why can they climb where no one else is able to go?" asked Carl.

"Behind each hoof there is another called the false hoof," replied the schoolmaster. "I looked at those of the dead chamois the hunter was carrying home. These extra hoofs give the creature the power to hold himself in places which would not be safe without their aid. Their bodies are very light and their legs are slim, while they seem to be entirely without fear of anything save men."

"Poor little things," exclaimed Franz. "We are taught to be kind to the birds and to protect them in every way. I never in my life knew of a Swiss harming a bird's nest. We ought to be kind to the chamois as well. I once knew a boy who had a tame one for a pet. His father caught it when it was very young. It was the dearest little thing, following its master about just like a dog. In summer its hair was yellowish brown, but in winter it grew darker and was almost black."

"Did you know that the chamois always have a sentinel on guard while they are feeding?" asked the schoolmaster.

"No, sir," said both boys together.

"Yes, it is true, the hunters have told me so. If this chamois guard hears the slightest sound or discovers even a footprint, he at once gives an alarm. Away flees the herd in search of safety.

"But, dear me! it is growing late and you must be up early in the morning. Then you must show me your store of cheeses," he added, turning to Carl's mother. "The cows are looking fine; they must enjoy the pastures here. And now, good night. May you all sleep well in the care of the loving Father."

In a few minutes every one in the little cottage was resting quietly.

CHAPTER IV

THE BRAVE ARCHER

It was a bright summer day. In the morning Carl's father had said to the boys:

"You may have a holiday and may go where you please with the schoolmaster. I will attend to the cows all the day."

So they had taken a lunch and had climbed to the summit of the mountain. Their kind teacher had told them stories of the flowers and the stones.

"They never seemed so much alive to me before," said Carl, as they sat resting on a big gray rock, far up above the pastures. "I like to hear you talk in school, dear master, but it is far better up here among the grand mountains and in the fresh air. Perhaps William Tell himself once stood on this very spot."

"It is quite likely," replied the schoolmaster. "You know that his home was not many miles from our village. He was never so happy as when wandering among the mountains. Those were wonderful times in which he lived. But there is the same feeling now as then. We Swiss love freedom best of all, and are ever ready to give our lives for it, if there be need."

"How cruel the Austrians were! They thought that because theirs was a large and powerful country they could do with us as they pleased. But they found themselves mistaken after awhile, didn't they?" said Franz.

"Yes, my boy, but never forget that our freedom started in the work of three men, and three only, who joined together with brave hearts. They worked with no selfish feeling, and, before the end came, they had filled all Switzerland with the daring to be free."

"Yes, yes, we will always remember that. And only think! one of those three men lived here in our Canton. I am always proud to think of it."

"Boys, look at our country now, and then turn back to the sad times long ago. Can you imagine the way those three men felt when they met in the dark night on the field of Rütli? Can you not see them pledging themselves to their country in throwing off the yoke of Austria?

"They hated their rulers so much that a peacock was not allowed to live in Switzerland. That was, you know, because a peacock feather was the emblem of Austria."

"Wasn't it about that time that William Tell lived?" asked Carl.

"Yes, and he was known through all the country as a brave man and a skilful archer. It was very natural that he should refuse to show honour to the Austrian governor."

"It makes me angry whenever I think of Gessler," cried Franz. "It seems to me only another name for cruel power. But is it possible that he really had his hat stuck up on a pole in the market-place of Altdorf, and that every Swiss who passed by was ordered to bow down before it?"

"I believe so, although some people think the whole story of William Tell is only a legend, and that is a part of it. Our history shows, however, that this brave man really lived."

"Won't you repeat the story?" asked Franz. "I love to hear it over and over again."

"Yes, if you like."

"After Gessler's hat had been stuck on the pole, William Tell was one of those who passed by. Bow before the hat of the cruel tyrant! It was not to be thought of. Tell took no notice of it whatever. He did not appear to know it was there.

"Now it happened that one of Gessler's spies stood near by. He watched Tell closely. He sent word to his master at once that there was one Swiss who would not give him proper honour. You know what followed, my boys. Tell was seized and bound.

"Gessler must have said to himself, 'I will make an example of this insolent peasant.' For Tell was brought before him and ordered to stand at a great distance from his little son and shoot at an apple on the boy's head. If he struck the apple he was to be allowed to go free.

"Do you think Tell feared he could not do it? No, he was too good an archer. But his child was so dear to him that his very love might make his hand tremble. Think again! the boy might move from fright, and then the arrow would enter his body instead of the apple on his head.

"It was a terrible thing to think of. But William Tell made ready for the trial. The time came. A crowd of people gathered to see the test. The boy did not move a muscle. The arrow went straight to its mark. The people shouted with joy.

"Then it was that Gessler, who had been watching closely, noticed that Tell held a second arrow.

"'Why didst thou bring more than one, thou proud peasant?' angrily asked the tyrant.

"'That I might shoot thee had I failed in cleaving the apple,' was the quick answer.

"'Seize him! Bind him hand and foot, and away with him to the dungeon!' shouted the enraged governor.

"His men seized Tell, and strong chains made the noble Swiss helpless. He was carried to a boat already waiting on the shore, for the dungeon was across the deep, blue waters of Lake Lucerne.

"Ah! how sad must have been the hearts of our people as they watched Gessler and his servants get into the boat and row away. They thought they would never see the brave archer again.

"But this was not God's will. A sudden storm arose before the party had gone very far. The wind blew fearfully, and the little boat was tossed about on the waves as though it were a feather. The rowers could not keep the boat in her course. It seemed as though, every moment, she would be dashed against the rocks and destroyed. Then it was that Gessler remembered that Tell was as skilful with a boat as he was with a bow and arrow.

"'Take off the peasant's chains,' he cried. 'Let him guide us to a safe landing-place. It is our only chance of being saved.'

"Tell was made free. His quick mind told him what to do. He seized the oars, and with strong strokes soon brought the boat close to the shore. Then, springing out, he pushed the boat off into the water.

"Would Gessler be saved? Tell wondered if it were possible. Then he said to himself, 'If the tyrant is not destroyed, he must go home through the pass in the mountains.'

"With this thought, he hurried up over the crags, and hid himself behind a great rock. He waited patiently. At last he heard footsteps and voices. His enemy was drawing near. He stood ready with bent bow. As Gessler came into view, whizz! flew the arrow straight into the tyrant's heart! He could never again harm Switzerland or the Swiss."

"Brave Tell! Brave Tell!" shouted Carl. "Dear master, have you ever visited the chapel which stands to-day in honour of this great countryman of ours?"

"Yes, Carl, and when you come back to the lowlands in the fall, you shall visit it with me. You and Franz must also go to look at the stone on which Tell stepped as he sprang from Gessler's boat. Even now, we can seem to feel Tell's joy when he wandered among the mountains, and thought of plans by which he could help his country. For after Gessler was killed, there was the whole army of Austria to be driven out."

"People needn't tell me that the story of William Tell and the apple is only a legend," exclaimed Franz. "I believe every word of it, don't you, Carl?"

"Indeed I do. Won't you tell us another story? Look! the sun is still high in the sky. We need not go home for an hour yet."

"Let me see, boys. Shall it be a tale of old Switzerland and of her struggles with her enemies?"

"Yes, yes," cried both boys. "We are never tired of hearing of the lives of our great men."

"Very well, then, you shall listen to the story of Arnold of Winkelried.

"It was a time of great danger. The Austrians were pouring into our country. Their soldiers, protected by the strongest steel armour, bore fearful weapons. Our people were poor, and had only slings or bows and arrows with which to defend themselves. What should be done? There was the Austrian army, closely drawn up, with shields glistening in the sunlight,—here were the Swiss, few and unprotected, but burning with love for their country.

"It seemed as though all chance of saving Switzerland was hopeless. Then the brave Arnold spoke.

"'Friends,' said he, 'I am ready to give my life for my country. I will rush into the ranks of our enemies and make an entrance for you. Be ready; follow with all your might, and you may throw them into confusion. You who live after me must take care of my wife and children when I am gone.'

"There was not a moment to be lost.

"'Make way for Liberty!' cried Arnold, then ran with arms extended wide, as if to clasp his dearest friend.

"A hundred spears were thrust toward him. He gathered as many as he could in his hands and arms. They entered his body on all sides, but before the hero fell he had made an opening into the ranks of the enemy through which his comrades dashed. Thrown into confusion, the Austrians fled, and were driven out of our loved country.

"Switzerland was saved for us, my lads, through the sacrifice of that noble man, Arnold von Winkelried. May you live to do him honour!"

"I can see him now, as he rushed into the midst of the cruel Austrians," cried Carl, jumping to his feet. "Noble, noble Arnold! I do not believe any other land has such a hero. Dear master, I will try to be braver and truer all my life, and be ready to serve my country faithfully in time of need."

"I, too," exclaimed Franz, "will be more of a man from this very moment."

"Well said, my dear boys. But come, it is growing late and you will be needed at home."

CHAPTER V

THE HAYMAKERS

"Mother! mother! here come the mowers," called Carl, as he came toward the house with a pail of milk in each hand. The wooden milking-stool was still strapped around the boy's waist, and its one leg stuck out behind like a little stiff tail. You would have laughed at the sight, as did the two haymakers who had by this time reached the hut.

"What, ho! Carl," said one of the men, "are you changing into a monkey now you have come up to the highlands for the summer?"

"I was so busy thinking," replied the boy, "that I forgot to leave the stool in the stable when I had finished the milking. I am glad you are here to-night. How does the work go?"

"Pretty hard, my boy, pretty hard, but I love it," answered the younger man of the two mowers. "Still, I shouldn't advise you to be a haymaker when you grow up. It is too dangerous a business."

"It isn't such hard work gathering the hay in these parts as it is in most places," said the older man. "Ah! many a time I have worked all day long on the edge of a precipice; it is a wonder I am living now."

"It is not strange that the law allows only one person in a family to be a haymaker," said Carl's mother, who had come to the door to welcome her visitors. "I am very glad my husband never chose the work. I should fret about him all through the summer. But come in, friends, and lay down your scythes. We are glad to see you."

The two mowers were on their way to higher places up on the mountain. They were cutting the wild hay which could be found here and there in little patches among the rocks and cliffs.

Could this work be worth while? We wonder if it is possible. But the Swiss value the mountain hay greatly. It is sweet and tender and full of fine herbs, while the higher it grows, the better it is. The cattle have a treat in the winter-time when they have a dinner of this wild mountain hay.

28

Carl's friends had large nets tied up in bundles and fastened to their backs. Their shoes had iron spikes in the strong soles. These would keep their feet from slipping, as they reached down over the edge of a sharp cliff or held themselves on some steep slope while they skilfully gathered the hay and put it in the nets. But, even then, they must not make a false step or grow dizzy, or let fear enter their heads. If any of these things should happen, an accident, and probably a very bad one, too, would surely follow.

When all the nets were filled, they would be stored in safe nooks until the snow should come. Then for the sport! For the mowers would climb the mountains with their sledges, load them with the nets full of hay, and slide down the slopes with their precious stores.

"May I go with you when you collect the hay in November?" Carl asked his friends. "I won't be afraid, and it is such fun travelling like the wind."

"It will take your breath away, I promise you," said the boy's father. He had come into the house just in time to hear what was being said. "I will risk you, Carl, however. You would not be afraid, and he who is not afraid is generally safe. It is fear that causes most of the accidents. But come, my good wife has made the supper ready. Let us sit down; then we can go on talking."

"How good this is!" said one of the visitors, as he tasted the bread on which toasted cheese had been spread.

Carl's mother did not sit down to the table with the others. She had said to herself, "I will give the mowers a treat. They are not able to have the comforts of a home very often." So she stood by the fire and held a mould of cheese close to the flames. As fast as it softened, she scraped it off and spread it on the slices of bread. Every one was hungry, so she was kept busy serving first one, then another.

She smiled at the men's praise. They told her they had spent the night before with two goatherds who lived in a cave. It was only a few miles away on the west slope of the mountain.

"They have a fine flock of goats," said one of the men, "and they are getting quantities of rich milk for cheese. But it cannot be good for them to sleep two or three months in such a wretched place. They look pale, even though they breathe this fine mountain air all day long."

"Carl and Franz don't look sickly, by any means," laughed Rudolf, as he pointed to the boys' brown arms. The sleeves of their leather jackets were short and hardly reached to their elbows. The strong sunshine and wind had done their work and changed the colour of the fair skin to a deep brown.

"You will have good weather for haying, to-morrow," said Franz, who was standing at the window and looking off toward a mountain-top in the distance. "Pilatus has his hood on to-night."

"A good sign, surely," said Rudolf. "We shall probably see a fine sunrise in the morning. You all know the old verse,

"'If Pilatus wears his hood,
Then the weather's always good.'"

The "hood" is a cloud which spreads out over the summit of the mountain and hides it from sight. Carl has often looked for this the night before a picnic or festival. If he saw it, he would go to bed happy, for he felt sure it would be pleasant the next day.

"I shouldn't think Pilatus would be happy with such a name," said Franz. "I wonder if it is really true that Pilate's body was buried in the lake up near its summit."

"That is the story I heard when I was a little boy at my mother's knee," said the old hay-cutter. "I have heard it many times since. It may be only a legend, but it seems true to me, at any rate."

"Tell it to us again," said Rudolf. "There are no stories like the ones we heard in our childhood."

"It was after the death of our Master," said the mower, in a low, sad voice. "Pilate saw too late what he had done. He had allowed the Wise One to be put to death. He himself was to blame, for he could have saved Him. He could not put the thought out of his mind. At last, he could bear it no longer, and he ended his own life.

"His body was thrown into the Tiber, a river that flows by the city of Rome. The river refused to let it stay there, for it was the body of too wicked a man, so it cast it up on the shore. Then it was carried to the Rhine, but this river would not keep it, either. What should be tried now? Some one said, 'We will take it to the summit of a mountain where there is a deep lake, and drop it in the dark waters.'

"It was done, and the body found a resting-place at last."

"You did not finish the story," said Rudolf. "It is said that the restless spirit of Pilate is allowed to arise once each year and roam through the mountains for a single night on a jet-black horse. On that night the waters of the lake surge and foam as if a terrible storm were raging."

"Are you going to the party to-morrow night?" asked the younger mower. "The goatherds told me about it. I wish we could be there, but our work is too far away. The villagers are getting ready for a good time."

"What party?" cried Carl and Franz together. They were excited at the very idea.

"Why, haven't you heard about it? You know there is a little village about two miles below the pasture where those goatherds live. The young folks have planned to have a dance and a wrestling match. I am surprised you have not heard about it. They expect all the herders and mowers to come from near and far. You will certainly be invited in the morning."

And so it was. Before the cows were let out to pasture, a horn was heard in the distance.

"Hail, friends!" it seemed to call.

Carl rushed into the house for his own horn and gave a strong, clear blast, then another and another. It was an answering cry of welcome and good-will.

A boy about twelve years old soon came into view. He wore a tight-fitting leather cap and heavy shoes with iron-spiked soles like Carl's. He came hurrying along.

"There is to be a party at our village to-night," he said, as soon as he was near enough for Carl to hear. "It will be moonlight, you know, and we will have a jolly time. All your folks must come, too."

Carl and Franz were soon talking with the boy as though they had always known him, yet they had never met before.

"My folks came near forgetting there was any one living here this summer," the strange boy said. "They only thought about it last night, but they very much wish you to come."

He stayed only a few moments, as he had been told to return at once.

"There is plenty to do, you know, to get ready for a party," he said. "Besides, it will take me a good hour to go back by the shortest path around the slope, it winds up and down so much. But you will come, won't you?"

Carl's father and mother were as much pleased by the invitation as were the boys. The milking was done earlier than usual, and the cows were locked up in the stable before the sunset light had coloured the snowy tops of the distant mountains.

It was quite a long tramp for Carl's mother, but she only thought how nice it would be to join in dance and song again. The wrestling match took place in the afternoon. The father would not have missed that for a good deal, so he left home three hours, at least, before the others. The boys stayed behind to help the mother in the milking and to show her the way to the village afterward.

The party was a merry one. They drank cup after cup of coffee, and all the good old songs of Switzerland were sung with a will. Carl's mother showed she had not forgotten how to dance. Carl and Franz were too shy to join in the dancing, but it was fun enough for them to watch the others. Oh, yes, it was a merry time, and the moon shone so brightly that it lighted the path homeward almost as plainly as though it were daytime.

"Next week we return to our own little village in the valley," said Rudolf, as the family walked back after the party. "Our old friends will be glad to see us as well as the fine store of cheese we shall bring. Then for another merrymaking. Carl, you must show us then what you learned at the gymnasium last year."

The boy's father was proud of Carl's strength and grace. "How fine it is," he often said to himself, "that every school in our country has a gymnasium, so that the boys are trained in body as well as in mind. That is the way to have strong men to defend our country and to govern it. I will buy Carl a rifle for his very own. The boy deserves it, he has worked so hard and so well all summer. He can shoot well already, and I will train him myself this winter, and in a year or two more he can take part in the yearly rifle match. I am very glad I have a son."

CHAPTER VI

THE MARMOT

It was the week after Carl got back to the village. What a busy day it had been for his mother! You would certainly think so if you had looked at the wide field back of the house. A great part of it was covered with the family wash. Sheets, sheets, sheets! And piece after piece of clothing! What could it all mean?

And did this little family own so much linen as lay spread out on the grass to-day? It was indeed so. In Carl's village it is the custom to wash only twice a year. Of course, chests full of bedding are needed to last six months, if the pieces are changed as often in Switzerland as they are in our country.

When Carl's mother was married, she brought enough linen to her new home to last for the rest of her life. Carl's grandmother had been busy for years getting it ready for her daughter. A Swiss woman would feel ashamed if she did not have a large quantity of such things with which to begin housekeeping.

When the washing had been spread out on the grass, Carl's mother went into the house feeling quite tired from her day's work. The two women who had been helping her had gone home. She sat down in a chair to rest herself, and closed her eyes. Just then she heard steps outside.

"It is Carl getting home from school," she thought, and she did not look up, even when the door opened.

"Well, wife, we have caught you sleeping, while it is still day. Wake up, and see who has come to visit us."

She opened her eyes, and there stood not only her husband and Carl, but a dear brother whom she had not seen for years. How delighted she was! He had changed from a slim young fellow into a big, strong man.

boy tied by a rope to a man, both climbing rocks of Matterhorn
CLIMBING THE MATTERHORN.
"O, Fritz, how glad I am to see you," she cried. "Do tell us about all that has happened. We have not heard from you for a long time. What have you been doing?"

"I have spent part of my time as a guide among the highest mountains of the Alps. There is not much work of that kind to do around here; the passes are not dangerous, you know. Most of the travellers who come to this part of Switzerland are satisfied if they go up the Rigi in a train. But I have taken many dangerous trips in other parts of the country, and been well paid for them."

"Have you ever been up the Matterhorn?" asked Carl.

"Only once, my boy. It was the most fearful experience of my whole life. I shudder when I think of it. There was a party of three gentlemen besides another guide and myself. You know it is the shape of that mountain that makes it so dangerous to climb. It reaches up toward the heavens like a great icy wedge.

"Of course, we had a long, stout rope to pass from one to another. It was fastened around the waist of each of us, as soon as we reached the difficult part. Our shoes had iron spikes in the soles to help us still more, while each one carried a stout, iron-shod staff. The other guide and myself had hatchets to use in cutting steps when we came to a smooth slope of ice.

"Think of it, as we sit here in this cozy, comfortable room. There were several times that I was lowered over a steep, ice-covered ridge by a rope. And while I hung there, I had to cut out steps with my hatchet.

"There was many a time, too, that only one of us dared to move at a time. In case the footing was not safe, the others could pull him back if he made a misstep and fell."

"Did you climb that dangerous mountain in one day?" asked Rudolf. "I thought it was impossible."

"You are quite right. We went the greater part of the distance the first day, and then camped out for the night. Early the next morning we rose to finish the fearful undertaking. And we did succeed, but I would never attempt it again for all the money in the world."

"O, Fritz, how did you feel when you had reached the summit?" asked Carl's mother.

"In the first place, I was terribly cold. My heart was beating so rapidly I could scarcely think. It was not from fear, though. It was because the air was so thin that it made the blood rush rapidly through the lungs to get enough of it.

"But I can never forget the sight that was before us. Everything we had ever known seemed so little now, it was so far below us. Towns, lakes, and rivers were tiny dots or lines, while we could look across the summits of other snow-capped peaks."

"Was it easy coming down?" asked Carl, "that is, of course, did it seem easy beside the upward climb?"

"I believe the descent was more terrible, my boy. It was hard to keep from growing dizzy, and it would have been so easy to make a false step and slide over some cliff and fall thousands of feet. I couldn't keep out of my mind the story of the first party who climbed to the summit of the Matterhorn."

"I do not wonder, my dear brother, the whole world sorrowed over their fate," said Carl's mother. "Only think of their pride at succeeding, and then of the horrible death of four of the party."

"Do tell us about it; I never heard the story," said Carl.

"A brave man named Whymper was determined to climb the mountain," answered his father. "Every one else had failed. He said to himself: 'I will not give up. I will keep trying even if the storms and clouds and ice-walls drive me back again and again.'

"He kept on trying, but each time with no success. At last Whymper formed a party with three Englishmen. They hired the trustiest guides known in the country, besides two men to carry the tents and provisions. After great trouble they reached the summit and planted a flag there to tell the story of their coming.

"But on their way down one of the Englishmen slipped. He struck the guide as he fell and the two men hung over the precipice. They were fastened to the others by the rope; surely they could be saved! But, alas! the rope broke under the sudden weight. Not only those men, but two others, were swept down four thousand feet!

"The others who were left were filled with such horror they could not move for a long while. Their skilful guide had been killed; could they descend the mountain safely now? It looked impossible; they were dizzy and faint. It seemed as though there were only one thing left: they would have to stay where they were till death should come.

"After a while, however, their courage returned and they succeeded in reaching the foot of the mountain at last without any other accident, but with a sad and fearful story to tell of those who started out with them."

"I should think we would have heard of your climbing the Matterhorn, Fritz," said Rudolf. "It was a great thing to do, and few have dared it. We are proud of you, indeed. How would you have liked to be in your uncle's place, Carl?"

"I wish I could have been with him, father. When I am older, I hope I may have a chance to do such daring deeds. I'll be glad to try, anyway."

Carl's mother shivered, as she quickly said:

"There are other kinds of brave deeds, Carl, which I hope you will be ever ready to do. Speak the truth and be an honest man in all things. That kind of bravery in you will satisfy me. But be willing for your mother's sake to stay away from icy mountain peaks."

The loving woman's eyes had filled with tears. Carl ran to her and put his arms around her neck.

"Don't fret, my dear mother, I will always try to do what you wish." And he kissed her again and again. As he did so, he began to cough.

"I believe Carl has the whooping-cough," said his father. "He never had it when he was little, and every now and then he gives a regular whoop."

"I wish we had some marmot fat; that would cure him quickly," said his mother. "At any rate, it would make him feel better."

"I have a bottle of the oil in my satchel," said his uncle. "It is good for so many things, I keep it on hand. Here, Carl, open the bag and take a dose at once. I got it from the fat of the last marmot I killed."

"O, uncle, I never saw one in my life. I've heard so much about marmots, I would rather hear you tell about them than take the medicine."

"You may have both the medicine and the story, Carl. While we sit around the stove this evening you shall hear of the fun I have had hunting the shy little creature."

Uncle Fritz was certainly good company. He helped Rudolf and Carl in doing the night's work about the little farm while the supper was made ready. Two or three of the neighbours came in after that. They had heard of Fritz's arrival, and wished to welcome him. It was a very pleasant evening, for Fritz was glad to see his old friends and had much to tell.

Before bedtime came, Carl asked his uncle to tell about marmot hunting. "You know you promised me before supper," he said.

"What shall I tell?" laughed Fritz. "You all know, to begin with, what a shy little creature it is, and how it passes the winter."

"It lies asleep month after month, doesn't it?" asked Carl. "The schoolmaster told us so."

"Yes, my dear. It lives high up on the mountainsides and close to the snow-line. Of course, the summer season is very short there. All through the long winter of six or eight months the marmot lies in his burrow and does not move. You would hardly call it sleep, though. The little creature scarcely breathes; if you should see him then, you would think he was dead.

"But as soon as there is warmer weather he begins to rouse himself. How thin he is now! At the beginning of winter he was quite fat. That fat has in some wonderful way kept him alive through the long months."

"Does he stay in this burrow all alone, uncle?"

"O, no. Marmots live together in families in the summer-time, and when the time comes for a long rest, a whole family enter the burrow and stretch themselves out close together on the hay."

"Where does the hay come from?" asked one of the visitors.

"Why, the marmots carry it into the burrow and line it as carefully as birds prepare their nests."

"I have heard," said Rudolf, "that one marmot lies on his back and holds a bundle of hay between his legs, while two or three others drag him through the long tunnel into the burrow. That is the reason the hair is worn off the backs of so many of them."

Fritz held his sides with laughter.

"Did you believe such a silly story as that, Rudolf? I thought you knew more about the animals of our mountains than that, surely.

"When a marmot's back is bare, you may know it is because the roof of his burrow is not high enough. His hair has rubbed off against it as he moved while asleep."

"How large do the marmots grow?" asked Carl. "Are they pretty creatures, uncle; and are they clever?"

"They are rather stupid, it seems to me, Carl, and they are not as pretty as squirrels. They are larger, however. The colour of their fur is a yellowish-gray. Their tails are short, like those of rabbits. They move about in a slow, clumsy way."

"Why are they so hard to catch, if that is so?" said Carl's mother.

"While they are feeding, there is always one of them acting as a guard. He stands near the opening into the burrow, and gives a cry of alarm if he hears the slightest strange sound. Then all the others scamper with him through the passageway into their home."

"But can't the hunters easily dig it out and reach them?" asked Carl.

"Sometimes the tunnel that leads to the burrow is many feet long. A friend of mine unearthed one that was actually thirty feet from the outside opening of the burrow."

"How did you manage to catch them? You have killed quite a number, haven't you?" asked Rudolf.

"Yes, I have been quite successful, and this is the way I worked: If I found any tracks or signs of their burrows, I crept along very softly. I kept looking ahead in all directions. Away off in the distance, perhaps, I saw something looking like a family of marmots asleep in the sunshine.

"I crept nearer and nearer. I must not make a sound or I would lose my chance. At last, when I was close upon them, I lifted a stone and blocked the opening to their burrow. Then I whistled. The poor little things waked up too late and saw that their way home was cut off. They gave a shrill cry, like a whistle, and fled together into the nearest cranny. There they cowered while I drew near and pinned one of them to the ground. It was an easy matter to end its life after that.

"If I wished to carry it home alive, I seized it by its hind legs and dropped it into a bag; the poor little thing was helpless then."

"You will stay with us for a while, won't you, Fritz?" asked one of the neighbours. "You have been a long time away, and have been living a rough and dangerous life as a guide. It seems good, indeed, to see you back again."

"Yes, I shall rest here for a month or so with my good sister and Rudolf. Then I must be away among my mountains again. I am never so happy as when I am climbing some difficult slope."

"It is growing late, friends," said one of the visitors. "We must bid you good night, for to-morrow brings its work to each of us."

"Good night, good night, then. But let us first have a song in memory of old days," said Fritz.

All joined with a good-will. Half an hour afterward the lights were out in the little house and every one was settled for a good night's rest.

CHAPTER VII

GLACIER AND AVALANCHE

It was cold weather now. Some snow had already fallen, and Carl had helped his father and mother in getting ready for the long, cold winter.

Uncle Fritz had been gone for quite a while, and the family had settled down to their old quiet life. One evening Carl was sitting by the big stove and telling his mother about the day's work at school, when the door opened, and who should stand there but Fritz. Carl rushed into his arms, exclaiming:

"I knew you would come back, because you promised, Uncle Fritz."

"Yes, but I shall stay only a day or two. Then I must be off again. There is a little village up in the mountains about twenty miles away. I must go there before the weather grows any colder, for if a big snow-storm should come up it would make hard walking."

"Will you go all the way on foot, uncle?" asked Carl. "I do believe you never ride in a train if you can help it."

Fritz laughed. "I must say I enjoy the walking best. But, anyhow, this time my way lies across country. How would you like to go too? I have to cross a glacier before I get there. Did you ever see a glacier, my boy?"

"No, Uncle Fritz, and I have always longed to do so. O, mother, may I go? I will study hard at school, and make up all the lessons I lose while I am away."

"How long will you be gone, Fritz?" asked his sister.

"Not over three days, if the weather is good; and after that I shall not stay in this part of the country. I am going to Geneva, so it will be Carl's last chance for a long time to go with me."

Man and boy looking at river of ice with full moon above
"IT WAS A RIVER OF SOLID ICE!"
In this way it came to pass that Carl went with his uncle.

"Do take good care of him, Fritz," the loving mother called, as the man and boy left the little cottage the next morning. "You know he is my only child."

"Never fear, sister. I will watch well, and try to keep danger away," Fritz promised.

Soon after the two travellers had left the village, the way became quite rough. Fritz told many stories of his wild life as a guide, and Carl was so interested he had no time to think about himself.

After three hours of hard walking, the two travellers stopped to rest and eat the lunch of bread and cheese Carl's mother had given them. A long tramp was still before them, and the way grew rougher at every step. The sun was just setting when the little mountain village at last came in sight.

It looked, at first, like a small bunch of black dots high up on the steep slope before them. But before it could be reached, the glacier must be crossed.

It was a river, indeed, but not like most other rivers in the world. It was a river of solid ice! When it first came in sight, it seemed like a broad, smooth sheet. Carl was a little bit disappointed. He turned to his uncle, and said:

"I don't see anything wonderful or dangerous in a glacier, I'm sure."

"Wait till you get a little nearer," was the answer. "It is not as easy to cross it as it at first seems."

"Why does it stay a river of ice all the time, uncle? I should think it would melt in the summer-time, and be like other rivers," Carl went on.

"High up in the mountains the snow stays all the year round. You know that?"

"O, yes, Uncle Fritz."

"Very well, then. The mass gets heavier and heavier, and much of it is gradually changed into ice."

"Yes, I know that, too."

"The great weight makes it begin to slide down. It comes very slowly, of course,—so slowly that it does not seem to move at all. But it does move, and brings with it rocks and trees and whatever is in its way."

"I see now why it is called a river of ice, uncle. But it doesn't move as fast in the winter as in the summer, does it?"

"O, no, it can hardly be said to move at all during the coldest months of the year. In the summer-time, however, it moves much faster than it seems to do. I have been crossing a glacier more than once when I was suddenly startled by a tremendous noise. It would seem like the roar of thunder; but as the sky was clear, it was certainly not thunder. It was a sound made by the glacier itself as it passed over uneven ground. It is very likely that deep cracks opened in the ice at the same time, making a noise like an explosion.

"But here we are, my dear, on the edge of the ice river. Don't you think now that it is a wonderful sight?"

"Yes, indeed. How beautiful the colour is! It is such a lovely blue. But dear me! look at this mass of rocks all along the edge. The glacier is a giant, isn't it, to make these great stones prisoners and bring them along in its course? They look strong and ugly, yet they are helpless in its clutches. It isn't easy walking over them, either, is it?"

After some hard climbing they found themselves on the glacier. It was not smooth, as Carl had at first thought, but was often cut into deep furrows or piled into rough masses.

"Look out, now, Carl. We must cross that deep chasm ahead of us very carefully. It is wider than it looks. Here! Follow me."

Fritz led the way to a place where the chasm was narrow enough for him to spring across with the aid of his mountain staff. Carl followed, while Fritz reached over from the other side and seized the boy as he landed. Carl laughed. He wasn't the least bit frightened.

"I think you did that because of what mother said, Uncle Fritz. You act as though I were a child, but I am very sure-footed and have been in slippery places before."

"No doubt of that, Carl. You are a brave boy, too. But it is very easy to make a misstep in such a place. I shouldn't like it very much if you were down at the bottom of that chasm at this moment. It wouldn't be easy getting you up again, even though it is not deep."

Here and there the two travellers met little streams of water flowing along over the surface. The day had been quite warm for this time of the year, the ice had melted a little, and the water was running off in these streams.

"O, uncle, look!" cried Carl, as they came near another chasm in the glacier. "Here is another bridge of ice over which we can cross. How clear it is; it looks like glass."

By this time the moon was shining in all her glory. "It is like fairy-land," said Carl to himself as he looked back at the glacier which they were just leaving, and then onward to the mountain-tops in the distance, lighted up by the soft yellow light.

"The mountains are God's true temples, aren't they?" said Fritz, after a few moments. "But come, my dear, it is getting late. We must move quickly now, even though we are tired. The lights in the village above us are calling, 'Hurry, hurry, good people, before we sleep for the night!'"

It had been a long, hard day, but Carl had enjoyed every moment. That night as he lay in the warm bed prepared for him, he thought it all over before he slept.

How kind these new friends were, too. Although he and his uncle had reached the village so late, a warm supper was made ready for them at once and everything done for their comfort. Why, the good woman of the house had even taken a hot stone from the hearth and put it into Carl's bed.

"I want you to sleep warm, my boy," she said, as she kissed him good night, "and it must be colder up here than in your own home in the valley."

The next day Carl had a chance to look around the little village. You would hardly call it a village, either. There were only six or eight houses. Their roofs were weighted down with rocks, like the cottage where Carl had stayed through the summer. It was the only way to be sure of safety, for the winter winds blew fiercely here; Carl knew that. There were long months when the cows must stay in their stable, week after week.

"But how neat the barn is!" exclaimed the boy. "It is almost like a sitting-room. Your father has a table and chairs here, as though he stayed here a good deal of the time."

"Yes, father likes his cattle so much, he wishes to be with them all he can," answered Marie, who was the only child in the house where Carl and his uncle were staying.

"Don't you think our cows are lovely, and did you notice the big black one in the first stall? She is the queen of the herd. Father let me name her, and so I called her 'Marie,' after myself."

"O, yes, I noticed her first of all," answered Carl. "I should think you would like it here better in summer than in winter. Aren't you ever afraid of avalanches, Marie?"

"Yes, indeed, Carl. Sometimes I lie awake and tremble all night. I can't help it. That is when the wind blows very hard and the house rocks to and fro. Then I think of the great drifts of snow above us on the mountain. What if they should start down and come in this direction! There would be an end of us; the whole village would be buried.

"Once last winter, I was wakened by a terrible noise. I knew what it was at once. It was an avalanche. It was coming this way with a sound like thunder. I ran into mother's room; she and father were on their knees, praying. The danger lasted only a few minutes and then all was still. But, do you know, Carl, in the morning we had sad news.

"The house of a neighbour had been carried away. His cattle were buried somewhere in the great snowslide and were never heard of again. But he and his family were safe because they happened to be spending the night with another neighbour."

"Was it a strong wind that caused the avalanche that night?" asked Carl.

"No, father said that could not have been the reason. But you know that sometimes even the cracking of a whip is enough to start the dry snow in the winter-time. Then, as it sweeps downward like a waterfall, more and more is added to it and in a short time it becomes a snowy torrent. O, it is fearful then!" and Marie pressed her hands together in fright at the very thought.

"You poor little girl. Don't talk about it any more. I'm so sorry I said a word about avalanches," said Carl. His voice was very gentle, because he felt so sorry for Marie. "Perhaps there won't be any more coming down this side of the mountain," he added. "Then you will be just as safe as I am in my home in the valley."

"Carl, Carl! where are you?" The words came from the direction of the house. It was Carl's uncle, who had wondered what had become of the boy. The children came hurrying out of the barn.

"It is growing dark, my dear, and I was afraid you had wandered off somewhere," said Fritz. "I promised your mother to look out for you, Carl, so you see I am doing my duty. Come into the house now. We will have a pleasant evening with our good friends. Then, with morning light, we must start on our homeward way."

That night many stories were told of the fairies and the gnomes. It is no wonder that when Carl went to sleep he dreamed he was living in a cave with the fairies, and that the gnomes brought him a pile of gold heavy enough to make him rich all the rest of his life.

CHAPTER VIII

SANTA CLAUS NIGHT

It was two weeks before Christmas. Carl had been back from his visit to the mountain village for more than a month. No harm had come to him on his way home, although heavy snow had fallen, which made hard walking. It was worst of all in crossing the glacier, but the boy's uncle took great care, and no accident came to either of them.

And now the joyful day had come which Carl liked best of all the year. He had saved up money for months beforehand to buy presents for his parents and his friend Franz.

What would he receive, himself? He thought sometimes, "I wonder if father will buy me a rifle. He thinks I can shoot pretty well now, I know that. But a rifle of my own! That would be too good to be true."

It was the custom of Carl's village to have the Christmas tree on Saint Claus's Day, two weeks before the real Christmas Day. They did not wait for the time at which we give the presents. Christmas was a holiday, of course, but it was somewhat like Sunday; everybody went to church. There was a sermon, and a great deal of music.

Saint Claus's Day was the time for fun and frolic. Good children looked forward to that day with gladness; but the bad children! dear me! they trembled for fear they would be carried off to some dreadful place by Saint Claus's servant.

All the day before Carl was greatly excited. He could hardly wait for night to come, but it did come at last. The supper-table was scarcely cleared before a loud knocking and stamping of feet could be heard outside.

Rudolf hurried to open the door, while Carl clapped his hands. Who should enter but a jolly-looking old fellow with rosy cheeks and twinkling eyes. He was dressed from head to foot in furs. Surely this was Santa Claus himself. There was a great pack of goodies on his back. Carl could see the red apples and bags of candy sticking out.

But who was the creature that followed Santa Claus? His face was black, his clothes were black, everything about him was black as soot. He carried a broom over his shoulder.

"This is my servant," said Santa in a big, strong voice. "I hope the child in this house has been good. I just called at a place where there was a boy who had not minded his mother. I was going to let my servant carry him off, but he promised to be good, so I forgave him this time." Santa Claus tried to scowl fiercely while he said these words.

"Have you been a good boy?" he cried, suddenly turning toward Carl.

"O, yes, sir, I have tried hard," answered the boy, who was half afraid, although, somehow, this same Santa Claus spoke very much like a friend of the family who lived near by.

"Very well, then." With this, Santa covered the floor with nuts and fruit which he shook out of his pack. A party of men who had followed him and his servant into the house, and were dressed up in all sorts of funny ways, laughed and joked with Carl's father and mother.

After a few moments of fun, Santa Claus went away, first wishing the boy and his parents good night and a merry day on the morrow. They had many more calls to make before their work would be done, and they must hurry on their way, they said.

When the door was closed, Carl said, "Father, I don't believe that is the real Santa Claus; it is neighbour Hans, who has dressed up like him. I knew his voice, too."

Carl danced around the room laughing, while his father and mother laughed, too.

"When I was a little tot," Carl went on, "I used to be scared, I tell you. I was afraid of doing naughty things all the year for fear mother would tell Santa Claus, and his servant would then sweep me away with his broom. Oh, I know better now." And Carl ran first to his father, and then to his mother, and gave each of them a hearty kiss.

The next morning, when he came downstairs, there was the dearest little fir-tree in the corner of the room, and under it lay some mittens and stockings, besides the rifle for which Carl had hoped and longed.

"Santa Claus helped me get them," said Rudolf, and they all sat down to breakfast laughing at the merry joke.

CHAPTER IX

THE WONDERFUL ABBEY

It was the beautiful spring-time, and the country had begun to look green and fresh again after the long months of snow and frost.

"Carl, my dear, how would you like to go on a pilgrimage to the Blessed Abbey?" asked his father one night as they finished milking the cows. "Easter Sunday is almost here, and the people of the village are talking of going to Einsiedeln together."

"O, father, that would make me happier than anything else in the world. What a fine time we can have! And only to think that I can see the place with my own eyes. Do you really mean it?"

"Yes, my boy, but do you think you can walk so far without getting tired out?"

Carl laughed. "Look at me, father; see how I have grown since last summer," and the boy stretched to make himself seem as tall as possible.

"Very well, then. Your mother knows about it, and is getting things ready for the journey now."

The next three days Carl could think of nothing else. He was full of excitement. The night before they were to start, he said to his father:

"Please tell me the story of the Wonderful Abbey again. I wish to have the picture still brighter in my mind as we journey along our way to-morrow."

Rudolf leaned back in his chair. His face was lighted by a happy smile as he said:

"Carl, my dear child, I love to think of the good souls who have made this world so beautiful by living in it. Yes, they have made it more beautiful than the grandest mountains or the loveliest lakes can make it.

"One of those good men was the holy Meinrad, who lived over a thousand years ago. He came from Germany to teach the priests at a small convent on the Lake of Zurich. After a while he said, 'I will live the life of a hermit in a little cell in the forest. I can best worship God if I live alone.'

"So he went up on the mountainside and made a hut, where he prayed and fasted day after day. It is said that the wild beasts felt his goodness, and would do him no harm. Whenever there was need, he went out to do good deeds among men. People heard of him through all the country round. They came to ask his advice when they were in trouble, or to seek help in other ways.

"But one day two robbers came to Meinrad's cell. They came with a bad purpose; they thought he must have a store of gold hidden away, and they wished to get it. The holy man gave them food and drink, but what do you think these wicked men did in return for such kindness? They cruelly murdered him! Then, finding no money, they hurried away.

"Meinrad had two birds who kept him company in the lonely forest. They were ravens, and had grown very tame, loving their master dearly.

"When the murderers fled, these birds followed them down the mountainside, across the lake, and into the town. The men stopped at an inn for food and rest. The birds flapped their wings against the windows, and kept up shrill cries. Every one in the inn wondered what it could mean. When this had kept up for several hours, the men thought, 'This is a warning to us from Heaven. We will confess what we have done.'

"They told the fearful story, and were put to death by the angry people who heard it. Ever since that time the place has been called the Ravens' Inn, and two ravens were carved out of stone and placed upon the wall. When we go to Zurich, Carl, you shall see those stone ravens, for they are still there."

"Now, please tell me about the holy abbey, father," said Carl, "and how it was blessed by the angels."

"After a while," his father went on, "the priests, who had heard the story of Meinrad's death, decided to build a grand church. It was to be on the very spot where Meinrad's cell had stood and he had been murdered. It was a beautiful building. When it was entirely finished, bishops and knights came to consecrate it to the Lord. People gathered from far and near to listen to the service.

"Now, it was the custom of the good Bishop Conrad to pray at midnight. On the night before the great day of consecration, he arose for his usual prayer, and, as he did so, was surprised to hear beautiful music in the air around him. He listened closely. Behold! it was the chorus of angels; they were consecrating the chapel. He bowed his head in wonder and awe.

"The next morning, when the people had come together for the sacred service, the bishop waited in silence till nearly noon, and then he told the crowd of listeners what had happened during the night. There was nothing for him to do now; the angels had already made this a holy place.

"But the people would not, could not, believe it. They still pressed the bishop to go on with the service. At last, he felt that he could not satisfy them in any other way, so had already begun, when a clear voice was heard to say, 'Brother, do not go on; for see, it is already consecrated.'

"Then the people were able to understand that the bishop had spoken truly, and the place was indeed a holy one now. Ever since that time good Catholics of France and Germany, as well as from our own country, make pilgrimages to the abbey of Einsiedeln. It is now a very grand building. Thousands and thousands of dollars have been spent to make it beautiful.

"And Carl, dear, you shall see there the very image of Jesus and Mary which the good priest Meinrad brought to the place when he first sought his home there. Better still, my boy, you shall drink from the fountain from which Jesus himself once drank, as I have been told."

Carl listened closely to his father's words. Others might tell him afterward that this was only a legend, but he was an earnest little Catholic, and believed that every word of it was true.

The moment of starting came at last. Rudolf, with his wife and Carl, was joined by several others of the village people. Franz was among them, together with his parents. There were many, many miles to walk, and several days must be spent upon the way. The nights were passed at taverns along the roadside. As our friends journeyed onward, they were joined by other parties, all going in the same direction,—to the abbey blessed by the angels.

In one party there was a blind man, who hoped to see again after he had drunk from the wonderful fountain. In another, there was a person who was lame, and who moved painfully along on crutches. He believed he would be able to leave these crutches behind him if he could once reach the abbey.

As Carl drew nearer and nearer, he could see that thousands and thousands of people were all going the same way. And now as they began to climb the mountainside, there were crosses at every turn in the road. He never passed them by without stopping to kneel and pray.

He was a stout little fellow, as we know, but he was growing very tired now. His feet were quite sore, and there were deep cuts in the soles. This showed that he had walked very many miles over the hard roads. But there were many others like him who had never travelled so far from home before; and some of them were old and feeble, too. He would not let his mother think he was tired. Oh, no, not for the world.

Ah! the spires were at last in sight, and every one hurried forward.

It was very, very beautiful, Carl thought, when he had passed through the great doorway, and looked upon the wonderful sight within. He had never before seen anything half so grand. The walls and ceilings were richly gilded, and there were many statues in the nooks and corners.

But best of all was the precious image of the Divine Child and His mother. It was only a clumsy-looking little wooden figure, and was black with age, but it was adorned with precious stones that sparkled brilliantly.

Before Carl entered the sacred building, he first stopped at the fountain, and drank from each one of the fourteen spouts. This alone would make his life better, he thought. But after he had received a blessing from the priest within the church, and had touched the marble on which the image of Jesus rested, he could go away perfectly happy.

There were many small inns in the village, and you may be sure that they were well filled at this time. Carl's family were together with their friends at one of them, and they had a merry time. When they were well rested, however, Carl's father said to the boy:

"We will take a trip to Zurich before going home. It is only a few miles away, and I promised to show you the stone ravens, you know. An old friend of mine lives right on the shore of the lake, and he will be glad to have us lodge with him."

Group of people on boat on lake
ON THE LAKE.
What a lively place Zurich seemed to the little country boy. Every one was so busy, and there was so much going on all the time.

"Why is it such a busy place, father?" asked Carl.

"It is largely because of the business in silk, Carl. We do not raise silk in Switzerland; it is too cold. But the cocoons are brought here from Italy, and thousands of people are kept busy in spinning, weaving and dyeing the precious stuff.

"The wife of my good friend is at her loom every moment she can spare from the work of her house. But she tells me the pay is very poor, yet the rich man who gives her the work sells the silk for great prices. Ah! it is hard to be poor."

Yes, it was true. Nearly every little home around the lake had its loom, and one could hear the whirr and the click in the houses as he passed along.

Carl took trips on the pretty steamboats on the lake. They had been built in the city and Rudolf took the boy to the shipyard where others were being made.

"All the iron steamers of Switzerland are built here," he said, "besides others which are sent to Italy and Austria. Yes, it is a great and busy place."

"Our schoolmaster told us once that people call these lakes of ours 'the eyes of the earth.' Don't you think that is a pretty idea, father? They are very bright and clear, as they lie walled in between the mountains.

"And, father, he says that there were people living on these lakes ages and ages ago. It was before any history was written, even."

"Then how do they know that such people lived on the lakes?" asked Rudolf.

"Whole rows of piles have been discovered under the water. Many were found right here in Lake Zurich. They must once have reached up much higher, but have rotted away!"

"Is that the only proof that people built their houses out over the water, Carl?"

"O, no, the schoolmaster says that many tools have been found in the beds of earth between the piles. They were almost all of stone. Besides these, there were things to use in housekeeping, and nets for fishing, and cloth, and even embroidery."

"Dear me! I never happened to hear of these strange people before," exclaimed Rudolf. "What name did the master give them, Carl?"

"He called them Lake-dwellers, because they built their houses out over the water."

"Does he know any more about them and why they chose such queer places for their homes instead of the pretty valleys or mountainsides?"

"He said it must have been in a warlike time and probably these people felt safer to dwell in this way. You see they could easily defend themselves in such places. Yet they had some farms and gardens, so they did not stay there all the time.

"They had very queer homes. The floors were made of round sticks, laid side by side. The chinks were filled in with clay and rushes. The roofs were made of straw and rushes put on in layers."

"How strange this all is. I don't really see how so much could be discovered," said Rudolf, half to himself. Then he went on, "I suppose they had no cows or other domestic animals, of course."

"O, yes, they had, father." Carl was proud to think he could tell his father so many things about them. "They had cattle, and sheep, and goats, and pigs; and they kept them in stalls in these lake dwellings.

"Why, only think! though it was three thousand years ago, probably, these people not only fished and hunted, but they spun flax and wove cloth. They made bread of wheat and other grains to eat with the fish they caught and the deer they killed. They must have known quite a deal to do that, even if they didn't write books to tell about themselves. Don't you think so?"

"Yes, Carl, I certainly think so. But come, it is getting late and we must go back to your mother and our friends. To-morrow we shall leave them and turn our faces toward our own little home. Are you ready for the long tramp?"

"Yes, my feet are tough now, and I don't believe they will get so sore as they did in coming. What a lovely time I have had. You are such a good, kind father to bring me here, as well as to the chapel of the holy Meinrad."

Carl looked up at Rudolf with such a happy face that his father bent down and kissed him.

THE END

57